FOR RICHARD, JORDAN, AND ALEX

ISBN-13: 978-0-9977220-6-2

A DartFrog Plus publication

DartFrog Books
PO Box 867
Manchester, VT 05254

www.DartFrogBooks.com

My mom has two jobs.

My mom is
a DOCTOR.
She figures out
why people feel sick.

And she's my mom.
When I fall down and get a bump,
she gets me a BAND-AID
and cleans me up.

My mom is
a TEACHER.
She helps her students
read and write.

AND SHE'S MY MOM.
WHEN I WONDER WHAT'S UP IN THE SKY,
SHE TEACHES ME HOW
THE STARS GO BY.

My mom is
an ENGINEER.
She uses math to invent
new things.

And she's my mom.
When I am bored, she says,
"let's take a trip."
Then she turns a box into
a ROCKET SHIP!

My mom is
a **POLICE OFFICER**.
She knows the rules
and keeps people safe.

And she's my mom.
When I take my friend's favorite
stuffed bear,

She teaches me to be HONEST
and to care.

My mom is
a **SECRETARY**.
She keeps the office neat
and on track.

And she's my mom.
When I can't find
my lucky SOCK anywhere,
she always finds it,
even under the chair.

My mom is
a DENTIST.
She makes people's teeth
healthy and clean.

And she's my mom.
Every morning and every night,
she helps keep

my TEETH shiny and bright.

My mom is
a **FIREFIGHTER**.
She climbs up ladders
and puts out fires.

And she's my mom.
When I reach for the outlet
in the hallway,
she shows me how

to be SAFE when I play.

My mom is
a NURSE.
She gives people shots
to keep them well.

And she's my mom.
When my stomach hurts,
she holds me tight,
and ROCKS me
until I feel alright.

My mom is
a LAWYER.
She fixes problems
when grown-ups fight.

AND SHE'S MY MOM.
WHEN MY BROTHER
DOESN'T PLAY FAIR,
SHE TEACHES US TO TAKE TURNS
AND TO SHARE.

My mom is
a WAITRESS.
She brings everyone
good food to eat.

And she's my mom.
When I am hungry and wearing a frown,
she makes me

The best SPAGHETTI in town.

My mom is

a **MILITARY SERGEANT**.

She protects our country and our flag.

AND SHE'S MY MOM.
WHEN IT'S TIME FOR ME
TO SAY GOODNIGHT,
SHE HUGS ME CLOSE
AND TUCKS ME IN TIGHT.

My mom is
a VETERINARIAN.
She cares for animals
that are hurt.

And she's my mom.
When my dog is wet and smelly,
She shows me how to clean his BELLY.

My mom is
a PILOT.
She flies airplanes
across the sky.

And she's my mom.
When I'm too tired
to walk anymore,

she picks me up HIGH
so I can soar!

Thank you mom, for the jobs you do.
You take care of me,
and make the world better too.

ABOUT THE AUTHOR

MICHELLE TRAVIS IS A LAW PROFESSOR AT THE UNIVERSITY OF SAN FRANCISCO SCHOOL OF LAW. SHE LIVES IN THE BAY AREA WITH HER HUSBAND, TWO DAUGHTERS, AND PET CHINCHILLA.